SCIFINITY

BUG TEAM ALPHA

THE
TIME VORTEX

by Laurie S. Sutton
illustrated by Patricio Clarey

STONE ARCH BOOKS
a capstone imprint

Sci-Finity books are published by Stone Arch Books
a Capstone imprint
1710 Roe Crest Drive
North Mankato, Minnesota 56003
www.mycapstone.com

Library of Congress Cataloging-in-Publication Data is available
on the Library of Congress website.

ISBN: 978-1-4965-5957-9 (library binding)
ISBN: 978-1-4965-5959-3 (ebook PDF)

Summary: The superpowered members of Bug Team Alpha are
engaged in combat when an explosion activates an ancient alien
time traveling device. Now half the team is trapped in 1600s
Japan — right in the middle of a samurai battle. Can the soldiers
find their way back home, without changing history forever?

Designer: Hilary Wacholz

Image Credits: Shutterstock: Mihai-Bogdan Lazar, throughout
(starfield), Somchai Som, throughout (Earth); Design elements:
Capstone and Shutterstock

Printed and bound in Canada.
010812S18

TABLE OF CONTENTS

Bug Team Alpha is the most elite special operations force of the Colonial Armed Forces of the Earth Colonial Coalition. Each member has an insect's DNA surgically grafted onto his or her human DNA. With special abilities and buglike features, these soldiers are trained to tackle the most dangerous and unique combat missions. Their home base is Space Station Prime.

Jackson "Vision" Boone

A human male with compound fly eye grafts. Eyes can detect multiple light spectra beyond human perception.

Rank: Commander
Age: 30 Earth Years
Place of Origin: Earth,
    European Hemisphere
Hair: Light brown
Eyes: Compound eyes
Height: 5 feet, 11 inches

Sancho "Locust" Castillo

A human male with bug wings and carapace grafted onto his back. He has immense strength and flying capabilities.

Rank: Lieutenant
Age: 23 Earth Years
Place of Origin: Earth,
    South American Hemisphere
Hair: Light brown
Eyes: Brown
Height: 6 feet

Irene "Impact" Mallory

A human female with a beetle exoskeleton grafted onto her body. She's always slightly hunched over like a linebacker ready to charge an opponent.

Rank: Lieutenant
Age: 24 Earth Years
Place of Origin: Earth, European Hemisphere
Hair: Red
Eyes: Brown
Height: 5 feet, 6 inches

Anushka "Spoor" Kumar

A human female with combination DNA from several scenting insects. Nasal cavity folds open to expose scenting filaments that can detect even the smallest percentage of compounds in the air.

Rank: Lieutenant
Age: 28 Earth Standard Years
Place of Origin: Earth Colony Amaranth
Hair: Brown
Eyes: Brown
Height: 5 feet, 5 inches

Akiko "Radar" Murasaki

A human female with cranial antennae grafted onto her forehead. She can sense vibrations and determine the distance between and shape of objects in dark spaces.

Rank: Lieutenant
Age: 28 Earth Years
Place of Origin: Earth, Asian Hemisphere
Hair: Black
Eyes: Brown
Height: 5 feet, 2 inches

Liu "Hopper" Yu

A human male with grasshopper legs grafted onto his hips. Footpads take the place of footwear. He is slender and always ready to jump.

Rank: Lieutenant
Age: 21 Earth Standard Years
Place of Origin: Earth, Asian Hemisphere
Hair: None, shaved head
Eyes: Brown
Height: 6 feet, 2 inches

CHAPTER 1

"This is a bad one, Jim. I need your help," said Commissioner G'dolen Suz of the Interplanetary Law Enforcement Agency.

General James Barrett, commander of the Colonial Armed Forces, sat in his office on Space Station Prime in orbit above Earth. He gazed at the image of his old friend on the monitor screen. G'dolen was from the planet Trimara and had the typical blue skin and triple amber eyes of her species. She and Barrett had known each other since they were cadets at the Military Academy.

Barrett didn't even wait to hear the problem. "What can I do to help?" he asked.

"As you know, the I.L.E.A. has been trying to shut down the illegal weapons trade cartel known as Starkshadow for years. They have hidden bases all over

Earth Colonial Coalition territory," G'dolen grumbled. "We've located a major Starkshadow base on the planet Rama 3. If the I.L.E.A. can capture it, we can end illegal weapons traffic in at least ten solar systems."

"So do you need Coalition troops? How many?" Barrett asked. He was already typing out the orders.

"My agents are excellent, Jim. I don't need soldiers," G'dolen said. "I need personnel who can think fast on their feet. Personnel who are experts in specialized operations like this one. I need Bug Team Alpha."

General Barrett nodded in agreement. He called up the file for available team members. The Bug Team was an elite, special ops force within the Colonial Armed Forces. They answered only to General Barrett and the president of the Earth Colonial Coalition. Not only were the soldiers of Bug Team Alpha trained for unique and unusual missions, their bodies were specially designed for it. Each member had a different insect's DNA surgically grafted onto his or her human DNA. This gave each of them superpowered buglike appearances and abilities.

Barrett selected a roster of six team members for the mission.

Commander Jackson "Vision" Boone. Compound eye DNA graft. Detection of multiple light spectra beyond human perception.

Lt. Irene "Impact" Mallory. Beetle exoskeleton DNA graft. High-impact tolerance and strength.

Lt. Anushka "Spoor" Kumar. Experimental combination DNA graft from several scenting insects. Nasal cavity folds open to expose scenting filaments and detect compounds in the air.

Lt. Akiko "Radar" Murasaki. Cranial antennae DNA graft. Vibration detection.

Lt. Sancho "Locust" Castillo. Wing and back carapace DNA graft. Heavy-duty flight and strength.

Lt. Liu "Hopper" Yu. Grasshopper DNA graft. Leaping ability.

"Send me the mission specs, and Bug Team Alpha will be on its way," General Barrett told the commissioner.

"Thank you, Jim. I knew I could count on you," G'dolen said.

"And you can count on Bug Team Alpha," Barrett promised.

✳ ✳ ✳

Twenty-four Earth Standard hours later, Bug Team Alpha and a squad of ten I.L.E.A. agents were in the middle of a fierce firefight on the planet Rama 3. They were exchanging fire with thirty Starkshadow personnel. The Coalition forces had pinned down the enemy outside four of the twenty weapons warehouses spread out on the secret base, which wasn't so secret anymore.

"Why did these crooks have to pick the north pole of an ice planet for their hideout?" Lt. Liu "Hopper" Yu complained over the comm to his teammates. He shivered despite his warm mission armor. Snow and wind swirled around the combatants.

"Because the north pole has a strong magnetic field. It blocks the base from sensor detection. Plus, the constant snowfall hides the warehouses from sight. Smart plan," Commander Jackson "Vision" Boone replied as he dodged enemy fire.

"So was hiding the base under this old structure. The ice and snow that's built up on the top provides excellent cover," added Agent Lyra Stardis, the leader of the I.L.E.A. team. "No wonder this place was so hard to find."

It had been ages since anyone lived on Rama 3. But a relic from the planet's long-vanished civilization still stood. It loomed above the cartel's warehouses. The struts of the huge metal structure arched over the entire base like the rib cage of an enormous beast. It was two hundred meters in length and a hundred meters tall. Layers of ice and snow had formed over the top and now acted like a canopy for the illegal warehouses.

Commander Vision looked at the frozen canopy above. With his large, compound eyes, he could spot tiny cracks in the ice. He aimed and fired his blaster at them. Chunks of ice broke away and crashed down on a squad of cartel members. Some of them were knocked out. The rest scattered.

"Bull's-eye!" Lt. Irene "Impact" Mallory cheered.

"Nice shot," agreed Agent Stardis over the comm. "But it's given the bad guys the same idea."

The criminals shot at the canopy above their opponent's heads. Ice rained down on the Bug Team and the law enforcement operatives. Agent Stardis and her team scrambled out of the way. It was difficult to move quickly in their bulky thermal gear.

Bug Team Alpha was quicker. They didn't need to wear heavy cold-weather gear. Their lightweight Talo-Titanium armor had built-in thermal pieces to protect them from the harsh environment. And their bug-DNA-enhanced abilities let them face the danger in their own unique ways.

Commander Vision and Lt. Anushka "Spoor" Kumar ran alongside the law enforcement agents. They held their weapons at the ready and blasted away any falling ice chunks before they hit the agents.

Impact shrugged off the falling fragments with her thick, buglike exoskeleton. She was built like a tank and was as tough as one. Lt. Sancho "Locust" Castillo was almost as strong. The carapace on his back that protected his wings acted like a shield against the ice.

Lt. Akiko "Radar" Murasaki easily dodged the largest chunks. She was using her cranial antennae to sense the vibrations of the ice falling through the air. Hopper leaped clear of the danger using his long grasshopper-like legs.

The teams regrouped behind a mound of boulders just inside the perimeter of the metal structure. "That dome of ice has become a problem. We have to get rid of it," Vision told Agent Stardis. "And I have an idea how."

"Let's hear it," the agent said.

"Bug Team Alpha goes in and blows up a couple of the weapons warehouses. The blasts should shatter the ice canopy and take out whoever is under it," Vision explained.

"Including the Bug Team," Stardis added.

"Don't worry about us. We'll get out in time," Vision assured the agent.

Stardis gave Vision a look that was half admiring and half skeptical. Then she nodded and turned toward her agents. "OK, team. Fall back!" she ordered. "Get out from under this structure!"

As the law enforcement agents retreated, Vision turned to the Bug Team. "Radar, Locust, and Hopper.

Target the southern warehouse. Impact, Spoor, and I will target the one on the north side," the commander instructed. "If you spot chemical weapons — abort. We don't want to poison the whole area. OK, set wrist computers for ten minute countdown to detonation, starting . . . now."

The Bug Team broke left and right. Hopper bounced through the swirling snow on his grasshopper legs. Locust buzzed into the icy air and followed behind. The cartel crooks fired at the two soldiers, but they kept ahead of the shots.

While Hopper and Locust distracted the enemy, Radar raced on foot toward the southern warehouse. Vision, Impact, and Spoor ran toward the northern warehouse unnoticed.

When Vision's team reached the northern warehouse, Impact slammed into the door. It fell off its hinges to reveal the interior. Containers were stacked from floor to ceiling. They were all marked with the universal symbol for explosives.

Lt. Spoor stepped inside. Removing her warm-air breathing mask, she opened her special nasal flaps and inhaled. Her sense of smell was far superior to the average human's. With it, she could identify what was in the warehouse. More importantly, she could identify what *wasn't* in the warehouse.

"I don't smell any chemical weapons in here," Spoor reported.

"Then we can safely set off some fireworks," Commander Vision said. He signaled his team to start placing grenades.

When they had finished setting the timers, the commander checked his wrist computer. Four minutes were left on the countdown. Right on schedule. Vision, Impact, and Spoor ran out of the warehouse. They took up a position beyond the perimeter of the metal structure.

"Vision to Radar. Report your status," the commander said over the comm.

"No chems. Charges set. Heading out the door now," Radar replied.

"Detonation is in two-and-a-half minutes. Get out from under that ice canopy," Vision urged.

"We've got plenty of time, sir," Radar assured him. Then she and her two teammates bolted from the southern warehouse.

Just like before, Hopper and Locust leaped and buzzed through a hailstorm of blaster fire. Radar used her antennae to sense and dodge all incoming blaster shots. She was so tuned in to the blaster fire that she missed something else. A cartel member had targeted the frozen canopy above Radar's head. A shard of falling ice was speeding straight toward her.

The ice struck Radar, and she hit the ground.

Her teammates heard her cry of pain over the comm. Locust turned back and buzzed at top speed toward his fallen teammate. Hopper leaped with all the strength in his grasshopper legs.

And then the warehouses blew up.

CHAPTER 2

A massive chain reaction of exploding weaponry rippled through the two warehouses. The explosions did what Bug Team Alpha had planned. Giant slabs of ice and snow began tumbling off the structure arching over the base. The cartel crooks stopped firing as they were flung backward by the explosion's destructive force. Then they started to run away from the frozen dome.

But the blast also caught two Bug Team members. Hopper was thrown mid-leap into an uncontrolled cartwheel. Locust was knocked out of the air like a swatted bug. They landed near Radar, dazed and motionless.

Hopper opened his eyes just in time to see a mass of ice plummeting toward them. "We're doomed," he groaned.

Suddenly everything went silent. The falling avalanche of snow and ice slowed until it seemed frozen in midair. Around the Bug Team, the air shimmered and turned a strange shade of blue. The ribs of the metal structure glowed with a vivid light.

"Or not," Hopper added.

Hopper felt his skin tingle. He looked at his hands. They were glowing a slightly deeper shade of blue than the bubble of air surrounding them. His whole body was glowing. So were Radar's and Locust's.

Radar struggled to sit up just as the bubble started to rotate like the vortex of a tornado. It spun silently, but the lieutenant bent over in pain.

"Aaagh! The vibes are so intense!" Radar moaned. She curled up her antennae and covered them with her hands.

The vortex began to contract around them.

"This can't be good," Locust said, just as the swirling sphere engulfed the Bug Team Alpha members.

A flash of white light almost blinded the three teammates. A few seconds later, the vortex started to expand.

Hopper blinked a few times. "OK, I'm glad that didn't kill us."

The vortex rapidly spun outward and dissolved. The Bug Team members braced themselves to once again face the falling ice on Rama 3.

But there was no icy avalanche. Instead, they were shocked to feel a warm breeze. They sat on soft grass and smelled . . . flowers? They barely had time to think about the switch in weather conditions. Armored warriors on horseback were galloping straight toward them!

"OK, now *that* might kill us," Hopper admitted.

"Evasive!" Radar shouted.

Locust grabbed Lt. Radar and buzzed into the air. Hopper jumped over the charging cavalry line. Unfortunately he was not able to look before he leaped. The result was chaos.

Hopper accidentally jumped into the middle of a troop of soldiers armed with swords and pikes. He barely avoided the sharp pikes and tumbled into a foot soldier. That soldier toppled into the one next to him, who got tangled up with the next one. The mass of soldiers began falling like rows of dominoes.

But Hopper wasn't the only one causing trouble. As soon as Locust buzzed into the air, the cavalry ahead of the troops was thrown into confusion. The horses reared and shied at the sight of a flying bug-man.

Locust held Radar and hovered above the chaotic battlefield. "What is going on?" he asked. "What's with the sudden change of scenery?"

"I don't know, but . . ." Radar trailed off as she got a better look at the troops below.

From their aerial viewpoint, Radar could see the warriors were all dressed similarly except for the tall banners strapped onto their backs. Each banner displayed a painted symbol along with elegant, fluid writing.

Radar gasped. "I . . . I recognize that writing. It's Japanese! And those symbols. They look like ancient family crests," she said. "Those warriors are samurai!"

"Whoever they are, Hopper is still down there with them!" Locust replied.

On the battlefield, the other soldiers were taking advantage of the confusion caused by the Bug Team.

They broke through their opponent's front line and plowed into the heart of their formation. Radar and Locust could hear the clatter of swords and the shouts of the soldiers.

"Hopper, report! Are you all right?" Radar asked over the comm.

The answer came in the form of several blaster shots. Radar and Locust watched as a dozen soldiers fell in a circle around a single combatant. It was Hopper. The remaining warriors backed away, shouting in confusion and alarm.

"I'm fine. Can't say the same for the opposition," Hopper replied.

"Something is wrong, really wrong," Radar cautioned. "You're fighting ancient samurai! We have to fall back and figure this out. Locust, grab Hopper and get us out of here."

Locust buzzed down like a swooping hawk and snatched Hopper from the circle of astonished warriors. They shouted in amazement and fear: "*Kami!*"

Radar recognized the word. In her ancestral Japanese language it meant "spirit." The soldiers thought Locust was a kami — a spirit.

"We need cover. Head for the forest on that hill," Radar instructed, pointing west.

Locust turned and sped toward the trees.

On the battlefield, the samurai continued their fight. The shock of the Bug Team's brief appearance had quickly worn off. It was only a short pause in the flow of the conflict.

However, a single warrior stopped to watch the man-bug fly away, carrying his odd companions toward the hillside forest. The warrior moved out from the fighting and then tapped something on his wrist. A drop-down sensor visor activated on his helmet. He hit the magnifying function. The three Bug Team members were revealed in sharp detail. He tapped another function and saw that they glowed with a bright blue energy invisible to human eyesight.

"Who are you, and what are you doing here?" he murmured in annoyance. Then he rode his android warhorse toward the western hillside.

Locust landed deep in the forest. The trees hid him and his companions from sight, but they did nothing to dull the sounds of battle on the open field below.

"This is definitely *not* Rama 3!" Hopper declared.

"Well, obviously! So where are we, and how did we get here?" Locust demanded. He had been on dozens of dangerous missions with Bug Team Alpha. But the events of the last few minutes had rattled his nerves.

"*How?* It was clearly that weird vortex!" Radar replied sharply. She had been thrown off-balance too. "As to where . . ."

Radar took a deep breath and looked down through the trees. The samurai troops battled on an open plain surrounded by tall hills. She felt something stir in her memory.

"I know this place," Lt. Radar whispered. Her face paled. "I recognize it from stories of my family's history. We're on . . . Earth."

"Great! So the vortex thing must have sent us home," Hopper concluded.

Radar watched the samurai armies clash with swords and pikes, cannons and flintlock rifles. Banners fluttered on the backs of the soldiers and cavalry commanders.

Then she saw a family crest that caused her heart to clench.

"Yes. The vortex sent us back to Earth," Lt. Radar said. "But the question we should be asking isn't *where* we were sent. But *when*."

Hopper nervously bounced on his long legs. "Wait, what are you saying?"

"I think the vortex sent us backward in time, into Earth's past," Radar explained. "I recognize the symbols on the banners. One in particular."

Radar pointed out a banner displaying a flowering vine called wisteria, curved into a semicircle. "That's the crest of the Murasaki clan," she said. "The crest of my ancestors."

Primitive cannon fire boomed up from the meadow below the Bug Team. The sound of musket shots popped. Bladed weapons glinted in the sunlight.

"There's only one place and one time we can be," Radar stated. "We're at the Battle of Sekigahara on the island of Japan. It happened in the Old Earth Calendar year of 1600 AD. We are hundreds of years from home."

CHAPTER 3

On Rama 3, Commander Vision led Spoor and Impact at a dead run outside the perimeter of the metal structure. The blast from the exploding warehouses almost knocked them off their feet. But Vision wanted to make sure that Locust, Radar, and Hopper had escaped from under the dome. He and his teammates sprinted toward the south end of the structure.

They arrived just in time to witness an alarming sight. Beneath the falling ice dome, a bright blue vortex of energy surrounded their other teammates. Then the vortex collapsed, and the three Bug Team members were gone. A second later, an avalanche of ice chunks buried the spot where they had been.

"Nooo!" Spoor shouted. She started to run toward the metal structure.

Blaster fire from the cartel criminals suddenly exploded at her feet.

"Fall back!" Commander Vision ordered.

The Bug Team reluctantly retreated. They took shelter behind a pile of boulders.

"What was that? What happened to Radar, Locust, and Hopper?" Spoor asked. She tried to look over the top of the boulders, but the cartel flooded the area with a blistering barrage of blaster fire.

Suddenly the furious blaster fire stopped. The only sound was the howling wind. Then a deep hum vibrated through the arctic air. Bug Team Alpha cautiously peered over the boulders.

They stared in amazement. The metal structure arching over the Starkshadow base was glowing. The ribs radiated from red to yellow, to a blinding blue.

Commander Vision watched the rainbow of colors with his enhanced eyes. "Aaagh! Those wavelengths are intense!" he said with a groan. He was forced to look away.

"Agent Stardis to Commander Vision. What's happening?" the I.L.E.A. team leader asked over the comm. Her voice was tense.

"I don't know," Vision replied. He didn't have any answers at the moment. Not about the structure, and not about where the rest of his team had gone. "Maintain your position."

The commander searched the surrounding area for the cartel. He had to focus on the immediate threat first. With his enhanced eyesight, he spotted the body heat of the enemy force. Several groups were scattered outside the perimeter of the base. They were hiding behind large snowdrifts and boulders, just like the Bug Team and the law enforcement agents. But everyone had stopped shooting to watch what was happening to the metal structure.

Horizontal beams of light appeared across the structure, forming a grid with the vertical ribs. The pattern looked like a huge, curved checkerboard. Hundreds of images flickered to life within the grid rectangles. Each one was like a monitor screen displaying a different picture.

Spoor pointed to one. "Look! It's Radar, Locust, and Hopper!" she exclaimed.

Not far from their rock shelter, Vision, Impact, and Spoor saw their teammates displayed on the energy grid. The image was still and motionless. But the

Bug Team could see that their friends were in an environment totally different from Rama 3.

"Where are they?" Vision yelled in frustration.

"Query received. Searching archives," a voice boomed from the metal structure. "The temporal coordinates are 31953-12155-3657."

The commander almost jumped in surprise, but the threat of enemy fire kept him behind the boulders. Instead, he peered around the side of the rocks at the glowing metal structure.

"What do you mean, *temporal*?" Vision asked the voice. "Are they somewhere else in time?"

"That is correct," the voice replied with no emotion. "They are at temporal coordinates 31953—"

"I heard the coordinates!" Vision interrupted. "But *where* in time are they? Are they on this planet? Be specific!"

"Searching archives," the voice responded.

"I think you're talking to a machine. An intelligent computer," Impact whispered to Vision.

"Agreed. That structure is more than just a hunk of metal, " Vision whispered back.

"Temporal coordinates match recorded travel to planet Earth. Country — Japan. Local date — October 21, 1600 AD," the voice said.

As the commander tried to process that startling information, the images on the grid started to move. It was as if someone had pressed play. The Bug Team watched Radar and her teammates face a charge of armored warriors mounted on horseback. They also saw what could only be dozens of other worlds and other times playing out before their eyes.

"Is this a time machine?" someone shouted. It was not one of the Bug Team.

"That is a primitive description. However, the answer is yes," the structure replied.

"Was that one of your people?" Vision immediately asked Agent Stardis over the comm.

"No," Stardis replied. "I think it was someone from the Starkshadow cartel. It seems they've taken an interest in this temporal tech."

The criminals unleashed a new wave of blaster fire at the law enforcement agents and the Bug Team. Vision, Impact, and Spoor ducked further behind the boulders.

"We absolutely cannot let them get their hands on that device," Vision said.

"Agreed," Stardis replied. "Do we blow it up like the warehouses?"

"No, not until I retrieve my team members," Vision decided. "I'm going to figure out how this time machine works and get them back."

A burst of blaster shots sounded over the comm as Stardis returned fire. "Oh. So you're a quantum engineer who specializes in temporal tech too? I guess that explains the 'special' in 'special ops,'" she joked.

Vision grinned. "Nope. But it seems like this computer likes to answer questions. I'll just ask how to use it," he replied as he and the Bug Team fired back at the enemy. "But first we have to take down these cartel operatives and secure the device."

"Commander!" Impact shouted. "It looks like the cartel is making a move."

"A group is running for the grids," Spoor added.

Commander Vision cautiously peered around the boulder. Four cartel crooks were sprinting toward the glowing metal structure. If they had hoped to run through the moving images as if they were video projections, they were wrong. All four disappeared in a burst of light.

"Whoa!" Agent Stardis exclaimed over the comm. "Did they just get vaporized?"

"Either that, or they've been sent somewhere in time," Vision replied.

"Hey, time machine! What happened to my people?" the cartel leader yelled out from behind a rock formation.

"They have been transported to temporal coordinates 53052-12757-5339. Planet Volcanis — equatorial region. Local date — one solar year before planetary destruction," the machine replied.

"Bring them back!" the leader demanded.

"Unable to retrieve. Travelers used an improper method of temporal transport," the machine said.

"What does that mean?" the man shouted angrily.

"Travelers must use temporal transport vortex to —" the machine began.

Commander Vision interrupted the voice by firing another round of blaster shots.

"Don't let the cartel get any more information out of that time machine!" Vision ordered over the comm. He turned to Spoor and Impact, who were hunkered next to him. "Pin 'em down! Keep 'em busy!"

Bug Team Alpha eagerly obeyed that order.

CHAPTER 4

Lieutenant Akiko "Radar" Murasaki looked down at the samurai armies on the plains of Sekigahara. She still could hardly believe it. She and two other members of Bug Team Alpha had been transported through time and space to Earth, to this important moment in the ancient history of Japan. It was also a part of her family's history.

Radar marveled at the sight of genuine samurai armor and weapons in action. When she was little, she had loved hearing the stories about her warrior ancestors. There was even a full set of antique samurai armor displayed in her grandfather's house. It had belonged to her many-times great grandfather, General Murasaki Akira. He had fought at the Battle of Sekigahara — the very battle that was unfolding before her eyes.

"This is so amazing," Radar said. "It's also extremely dangerous."

"Dangerous?" Locust repeated. "Why? We have the better weaponry — blasters, high-yield grenades, Talo-Titanium armor . . ."

"Not to mention our bug powers," Hopper added, bouncing lightly on his footpads like a boxer ready to fight. "We can take care of ourselves."

"I meant that it's dangerous for us to be *here*, in the past," Radar explained. "Anything we do could change history."

"Oh. Do you mean like that old story of the guy who goes back in time and accidentally kills his own father, so then the guy wasn't even born?" Locust asked.

"Yeah! But then how could the guy even exist to go back in time in the first place?" Hopper added.

"Because he erased his own timeline," Radar replied. "Like I said, this is dangerous."

Locust sighed. "Ugh . . . time travel theory makes my head hurt."

"Just remember that any change, no matter how small, could affect the future. The results could be disastrous," Radar told them. "We have to be careful."

The three teammates looked out at the battling samurai armies. They all knew Bug Team Alpha was hundreds of years out of place.

"Excuse me, but what are you doing here?" a new voice said.

The Bug Team spun around and aimed their blasters. A figure in samurai armor mounted on a warhorse faced them.

The samurai held up his hands. "Easy! There's no need for violence!"

Radar's antennae twitched. "I'm getting vibes of a visual distortion field. That's not a samurai — that's tech!" she told her teammates.

Locust's grip tightened on his blaster. "Who are you?" he demanded.

"I'm an authorized temporal scholar, and you are interfering with the timeline," the samurai replied.

The man tapped something on his wrist, and the image of the samurai warrior dissolved. It revealed a small humanoid male with sleek, catlike features. He was dressed in a jumpsuit that had dozens of pockets. Each one was bulging. Two satchels hung over his shoulders in a crisscross. The satchels were bulging too.

"You have very full pockets for a scholar," Radar observed suspiciously.

"I'm authorized!" the fellow replied, offended. "I'm allowed to be here, but you are not. Explain yourselves, or I'm going to report you!"

"Sorry, but time travel isn't normal where we come from — I mean, *when* we come from. This is confusing," Radar admitted, lowering her blaster. "Look, we don't want to be here, but we don't know how to get back."

"Well, that's silly. You simply go back the same way you came," the scholar told her. "Wait. How *did* you get here?"

"A blinding blue vortex," Hopper said.

The scholar pulled a small sensor device from a pocket. He pointed it at the Bug Team. "Well, that explains the blue energy residue in your bodies," he said as he examined the readings. "But I don't know of any planet in the Temporal Accord that uses a vortex as temporal transport."

"Temporal Accord? I've never heard of such a thing. Who are you?" Radar asked.

The scholar slid off his large android horse. He bowed politely to Radar, Locust, and Hopper in turn.

"I am Professor Liin," the man said proudly. "Dean of Ancient War and Weapons Studies at Waazda University on Zurvan—"

Before he could finish, a group of samurai emerged from the thick forest. They charged toward the Bug Team and the professor with swords at the ready. Locust and Hopper immediately aimed their blasters.

Radar held out a hand. "Don't —"

BZZZZAAAAT! Locust and Hopper fired their weapons, and the samurai fell to the ground.

"— shoot," Radar finished. She turned to her teammates with a scowl.

"It was set on stun!" Locust protested.

"*Anything* we do could affect the timeline!" Radar reminded him. "Those samurai might have had something important to do later in the battle."

"Actually, you haven't made a blip," Professor Liin assured them. He showed the Bug Team his computer tablet. Graphs and charts scrolled smoothly across the screen. No blips.

Radar still glared at Locust and Hopper. "Then we were lucky."

"Or, maybe you're meant to be here. Maybe you're already part of the timeline," Liin said. "It is possible that I've never noticed you before."

"Just how many times have you been here?" Locust asked.

The scholar chuckled. "Oh! Dozens — literally!"

"Well, it makes me nervous to be here at all. I'm watching my own family history," Radar said as she gazed down at the Battle of Sekigahara.

"Wait. What?" Professor Liin said, looking up from his computer displays. "Did you say *family* history? Oh no. That could change the —"

The professor was interrupted by the sound of more samurai stomping through the forest. The Bug Team's blaster shots had alerted a nearby war camp.

"Evasive!" Radar said.

Locust wrapped his arms around both his teammates and buzzed into the air. Radar reached for the professor.

"He can carry all of us!" she told the scholar.

"He doesn't have to," Professor Liin said as he tapped something on his wrist. He suddenly shimmered and took on the appearance of a samurai. "Fly! I will find you later!"

As Locust buzzed out from the cover of the forest, a musket shot rang out. He groaned and faltered in the air.

"I'm hit," Locust gasped. His grip loosened on his teammates. The small musket ball had found its way between the joints of the Talo-Titanium armor that covered his leg.

"Hang on, buddy," Hopper encouraged. "Find somewhere to land, and we'll get you patched up."

The trio flew above the raging battlefield. Locust searched for a safe place to set down, but there wasn't one. The ground was covered with combatants. Locust started to lose altitude. In a few moments they would land, whether they liked it or not.

Radar knew they had only one choice. "There! Head over there!" she shouted, pointing north. "Head for the Red Devils!"

Locust and Hopper looked north. A group of samurai dressed in blood-red armor was fighting another troop of soldiers.

Hopper frowned. "Are you sure? They don't look very friendly."

"They're allies of the Murasaki," Radar said.

"How do you know that?" Hopper asked.

"Family history," Radar reminded them. "I'll explain more later. Right now they're our only hope."

So amid booming cannons and clanging swords, Locust descended shakily toward the Red Devils.

CHAPTER 5

On Rama 3, Bug Team Alpha and the Interplanetary Law Enforcement Agency operatives continued their battle against the members of the Starkshadow cartel. Bright blaster fire pierced the dark and gloomy winter landscape.

The six-member Bug Team was down three teammates. The I.L.E.A. team was still at full strength with ten agents. Commander Vision peered around the boulder he was using for cover. With his enhanced eyesight, he spotted the body heat of the cartel members through the swirling snow. They were running toward a large rock formation. He counted twenty. There had been thirty.

Vision knew that four had disappeared into the time grid. That meant six were missing. It was possible they had not escaped the structure after the explosion. Or they could be hiding inside one of the eighteen warehouses that were still standing. Or, maybe they had stepped through one of the time portals. There were many possibilities, but no way to know for sure.

The only thing for certain was that twenty cartel crooks had just found a secure shelter. They were now hunkered under a large rock formation with an overhang. Big boulders also protected the sides. The shelter was as snug as a cave. Bug Team Alpha and I.L.E.A. were still out in the snow in near-blizzard conditions.

"We've got a standoff situation. It's like a siege. We can't get in, but they can't get out," Commander Vision said. "Who can outlast the other?"

"Whoever has the most ammo," Impact replied.

Bug Team Alpha and the I.L.E.A. team fired off a series of blistering rounds at the shelter. Rock shards flew off the overhang and surrounding boulders. The enemy quickly responded in kind.

"I'm down to two power packs," Impact told the commander. She slapped a new power cartridge into her blaster.

"I've got three," Spoor added.

"I've got three, but I'll be down to two in about a minute," Vision said. "Agent Stardis, what's your ammo situation?"

"We're getting low," the I.L.E.A. team leader replied over the comm. "Any suggestions?"

Impact shrugged. "Explosives are always good."

"Hmm. We could plant charges on the overhang and cause a rock fall. They'd be trapped inside. I like it," Stardis replied. "How about you, Commander?"

"It's simple and effective. I like it too," Vision said. "Impact, would you do the honors?"

Impact grinned. "Gladly."

Spoor shuffled over, making sure to stay crouched below the boulders. "Sir, I request permission to provide backup," she said.

"Permission granted," Vision replied.

Enemy blaster fire followed Impact and Spoor as they sprinted across the open terrain. Snow swirled around them. The white flakes masked them from visual sight, but the cartel had excellent weapons tech that detected body thermals.

Impact and Spoor ran in a zigzag pattern and returned fire. Their I.L.E.A. allies provided additional cover fire. It forced the cartel criminals to the back of the shelter. Impact and Spoor were able to dash to the rear of the snow-covered rock formation. They climbed onto the overhang.

Impact unhooked several grenades from her combat belt. "Two right, two left, two in the middle," she said.

Spoor did the same. They set the grenades and timers at the front of the rock formation. Then they ran. Their wrist computers chimed just before detonation.

BAAAAALAAAAAM!

The force of the explosion knocked Spoor off her feet. Impact reached out an arm and caught her teammate. Then Impact pressed Spoor against her body, tucking and rolling along with the blast. Flying chunks of ice and rock bounced off Impact's hard exoskeleton. The two tumbled at least twenty meters.

Vision watched from his position as Impact and Spoor finally came to a stop. They looked like a giant snowball. It didn't move.

"Impact! Spoor! Report!" Commander Vision shouted over the comm.

There was no response.

"Bug Team Alpha, report! That's an order!" Vision repeated.

The comm was muffled. "Uhhh . . . Bug Team Alpha reporting," Lt. Impact groaned. She relaxed her arms, and the snowball fell apart around her.

"Bug Team . . . reporting too," Spoor mumbled as she fell out of Impact's protective hold.

"We're OK, sir. Mission success?" Impact asked.

There was a long silence. "Negative. Mission failure," the commander finally replied. "It appears the rock shelter is fortified."

"What?!" Impact shouted. She jumped to her feet as if she had never been stunned by the blast.

"The grenades destroyed the rock overhang, but there's a metal structure underneath," Vision explained. "It must be a secret shelter the cartel set up outside of the base. The siege shelter has not been breached."

"Spoor and I are still in position behind them," Impact said. "We can try again."

"Negative. Find cover and wait for instructions," Vision ordered.

"Yes, sir," Impact and Spoor replied. The teammates looked around at their snow-blown surroundings. There was no shelter in sight.

Impact turned toward Spoor with a wicked smile. "I don't see any cover, do you?" she said. Impact started to walk back toward the destroyed rock overhang.

"Why are you smiling?" Spoor asked cautiously as she followed Impact.

The two returned to what was left of the overhang. They got down on their stomachs and crawled to the ledge. When they looked under it, they saw the front of a tough metal transport container. It was similar to the ones they had seen in the weapons warehouses.

"There's a nice, fortified shelter right under our feet. I think we should take cover there," Impact suggested.

Spoor grinned too. "You're right. But we're going to have to kick out the bad guys first."

The teammates split up. They worked their way down opposite sides of the jumble of boulders toward the ground.

"Impact! Spoor! I can see your body thermals. What are you doing?" Commander Vision asked over the comm.

"Taking cover, sir," Impact replied innocently.

"Just following orders, sir," Spoor added.

"That's not what I meant, and you both know it," Vision said.

"Commander, we have a chance to breach the siege shelter. It's exposed, and Spoor and I are in position," Impact argued. "Let us do this. We can capture the bad guys, and then focus on getting our teammates back from wherever they are."

The two lieutenants could hear Vision sigh over the comm. "Very well. Proceed with caution," he said.

"'Caution' is my middle name!" Impact replied.

"Ha!" Spoor snorted as she set a grenade. "I don't believe that for a second."

"You're right. My middle name is *ruuuun*!" Impact yelled as she activated the last grenade timer.

The two teammates sprinted in opposite directions away from the fortified shelter. The timers hit zero.

BWAAAM! BLAAAAM!

As Impact ran from the blast, rock shards came flying toward her. But her tough exoskeleton protected her from the sharp chunks.

Spoor was once again caught by the blast, but she was not protected by her teammate this time. The force pushed her headfirst into the ground. The impact ripped away her protective breathing mask and shoved snow into her sensitive nasal cavities. The burst of extreme cold caused Spoor's respiratory system to go into shock. Everyone on the comm system heard her groans of distress.

"Spoor! Report!" Commander Vision demanded over the comm.

Vision leaned out from behind the protection of the boulders. His action didn't draw any bursts of enemy fire. The commander scanned the cartel's position, searching for Spoor's distinct body-heat signature. The area was covered with thick smoke.

"All I.L.E.A. personnel, move in. Extreme caution," Vision instructed.

"Moving in," Stardis replied. Her operatives moved toward the destroyed cartel shelter in a wide sweep.

Commander Vision ignored his own order for caution. He ran toward the faint body-heat signature lying in the snow.

CHAPTER 6

Locust hit the ground heavily as his wounded leg gave out from under him. Radar and Hopper quickly got to their feet. They had to. They had landed behind a troop of samurai known as the Red Devils.

The soldiers dressed in blood-red armor were busy engaging the front line of their enemy. They didn't notice the strange-looking Bug Team at their rear. But the troop's general spotted them. He galloped over.

The general barked out an angry question. Then his eyes flicked to the Bug Team's armor and DNA enhancements. He unsheathed a long sword.

Locust and Hopper exchanged a look. They didn't know the man's language, although it was clear they were in trouble. But Radar understood. She fell to her knees and bowed before the mounted warrior.

"Honorable general! Lord Ii Naomasa! I'm Murasaki Akiko," Radar replied in Japanese, her ancestral language.

"Murasaki?" the general repeated.

"Yes, great lord. I have lost my way. Where is the Murasaki camp?" Radar asked.

Lord Ii pointed his sword toward a hillside covered with banners carrying the wisteria symbol. Then he growled, as if annoyed his battle had been interrupted to give directions. He galloped away to rejoin his troop.

"How did you know who that guy was?" Hopper asked.

"Like I said, family history. I know this battle and the people involved," Radar replied. She looked around at their surroundings. All was calm, but that could change at any moment. "I'll explain, but first let's get off the battlefield. Also, you should both set your comm units to translate Japanese. I'll do the talking, but then you can at least understand what people are saying."

After Hopper and Locust adjusted their comm units, Radar led the way to the Murasaki war camp. Right now, it was the safest place to recover and figure out a plan. She and Hopper supported Locust as they walked. The dead were sprawled all around them. Radar leaned down and pulled a piece of silk fabric from the waist of a corpse.

"*Gomen.* Sorry," Radar apologized to the fallen soldier. She took a clean pressure bandage from her emergency medical pack and placed it on Locust's wound. She wrapped it with the silk fabric.

Locust gripped Radar's wrist. "So, about that family history . . . What's going on here?"

"All right. Family history, the short version," Radar said with a sigh. "The Battle of Sekigahara was an important battle during this time period. It would help determine who would control Japan. My ancestors, the Murasaki clan, fought on the side of Lord Tokugawa Ieyasu. One of his allies was Ii Naomasa, leader of the Red Devils. They were hard to miss and hard to forget. I heard stories about them all through my childhood."

Radar stopped and ripped a strip of cloth from a banner on the ground. She wrapped it around her forehead to hide her antennae. Then she cut a section of shoulder armor from a fallen samurai and draped it over her Talo-Titanium gear. The Bug Team would have to blend in if they wanted to get into the Murasaki war camp without drawing attention to themselves.

"*Gomen*," she murmured.

Hopper and Locust took the hint. They began picking up pieces of samurai armor to disguise themselves.

"*Gomen*," they whispered.

"Lord Tokugawa's army of eastern clans fought the western clans loyal to Lord Toyotomi Hideyori here at Sekigahara," Radar continued. "The stories about the battle are filled with epic fights and mysterious kami spirits. There were even ninja who tried to assassinate my many-times great grandfather, General Murasaki Akira. Of course, most of that stuff has been exaggerated over the centuries. But the legacy of Murasaki Akira inspired me to have a military career."

"Wow. So, who won here?" Hopper asked.

"Tokugawa, which was lucky for the Murasaki clan," Radar replied. "The clans on the losing side lost their lands, their heritage. My family kept everything."

Radar fixed her gaze on the Murasaki banners. "I don't want to do anything to mess that up," she said.

The Bug Team continued toward the hill. Along the way they covered themselves with more samurai armor.

Just then, an injured soldier sprawled on the ground nearby reached out a hand. "Help," he gasped.

Locust did not hesitate. Despite his own wound, he pulled away from his teammates and helped the samurai get to his feet. They leaned on each other and limped toward the camp. Radar gave him a stern look.

"I know — we need to protect the timeline," Locust whispered. "But I can't refuse a soldier asking for help."

Radar sighed, but she nodded. Locust was right. Leaving behind an injured soldier would betray their military code of conduct.

By the time the Bug Team reached the Murasaki war camp, they had several wounded samurai with them. But as they entered the camp, a pair of perimeter guards spotted them. They stopped the group.

"Who are you?" one of the guards demanded.

The wounded samurai fell to their knees and bowed. They all gave their names in a rush. Only Radar and the Bug Team stood straight.

"And what kind of freak are you?" the other guard sneered as he looked up at Hopper's extremely tall form.

Hopper leaned down toward the samurai's face. Radar saw the defiant glint in her teammate's eyes. If a fight broke out, it would call attention to the Bug Team — attention they did not want. She had to take control of the situation and calm things down. Fast.

"*Yoshinasai!* Stop it!" Radar declared, stepping forward. "I am Murasaki Akiko. He is my bodyguard! You will treat him with respect!"

"*A-Akiko Hime?* Princess Akiko?" the guard gasped. "Forgive me, I did not recognize you."

Radar knew she had been named for an ancestor from this era. The other Akiko was a lady-in-waiting in the Imperial Court. But Radar didn't know she looked like her!

The lieutenant realized this could be an advantage. Radar took another step forward. She gestured to her scavenged armor in a display of disgust.

"I have been forced to wear this dirty armor to escape the battlefield. If it weren't for my brave protectors, I would be dead! Now, someone take us to the medical tent immediately!" Radar demanded.

"*Hai!* Yes!" the guards shouted. One of them waved at a passing camp servant. "You! Take these people to the medical tent!"

Radar led her band of wounded samurai and teammates into the war camp. She wasn't too far away when she heard one of the guards call out:

"Tell Lord Murasaki Akira that the princess is here!"

"What was that about not messing up the timeline . . . princess?" Hopper whispered.

CHAPTER 7

On Rama 3, Commander Vision dropped to his knees next to his fallen teammate. Lt. Spoor lay unmoving in the snow several meters from the smoking ruin of the cartel shelter.

The law enforcement agents moved toward the shelter with blasters ready, but there was no struggle. Everything was eerily quiet after the firefight of the last few hours. Only the wind moaned. And so did Lt. Spoor.

"Spoor! Are you all right?" Vision asked as he pulled his soldier from the snow.

The lieutenant came to her senses, but she immediately wished she hadn't. Spoor's skull felt like it was burning from the inside. Snow had been forced into her sensitive nasal cavities. She tried to lift her hands to her face, but they were shivering too violently.

Commander Vision saw the packed snow around Spoor's nasal flaps and realized what must have happened. He dug into his emergency medical pack and pulled out a thermal pad. He slapped it between his palms to activate it and placed it over the bridge of the lieutenant's nose.

Spoor sighed. The heat brought instant relief.

"Spoor! Are you all right?" Impact yelled as she thundered over to her teammate.

"Am I in an echo chamber?" Spoor rasped. Then she fell into a fit of coughing.

"Impact, get her back to the ship," Vision ordered. "She needs medical attention."

Spoor's eyes widened. She shook her head forcefully in protest. It made her dizzy, but she struggled to her feet and stood upright. She wobbled a little, but Commander Vision understood her message.

Vision sighed. "Fine, you can stay. But at the first sign of complications, you're going to the medical bay."

"Don't worry. I'll keep her out of trouble," Impact said. She wrapped an arm around Spoor's shoulders. Spoor was almost knocked over by the friendly gesture.

"Thanks," Spoor replied in a choked whisper.

"Now let's go see what kind of damage you've done to that siege shelter," the commander said.

The Bug Team walked through the swirling snow to what was left of the shelter. The rock around the entrance was now just a pile of pebbles. The metal structure underneath had been ripped open from the Bug Team's second round of explosives.

They looked inside. Agent Stardis and the other I.L.E.A. operatives were putting handcuffs on the dazed cartel members. The fight had been knocked out of the enemy. They had surrendered easily. Commander Vision did a head count — eighteen.

"There should be twenty," Vision said.

Agent Stardis looked over at the commander. "What?" she asked sharply.

"There should be twenty cartel guys in here," Vision repeated. "Two are missing."

Stardis frowned. "They must have escaped just after the blast, before we moved in. And there's no way to track their footprints in this windblown snow."

"But there's nowhere else for them to go," Impact pointed out. "Unless they have another hidden shelter like this one."

"They could have an escape ship somewhere," Spoor suggested. "They might try to leave the planet."

"If they get away, they'll tell their bosses about the time travel device," Vision warned. "The Starkshadow cartel must not get their hands on this tech. Who knows what kind of trouble they could cause?"

"I agree," Stardis said. "Don't worry, my team will find them."

Vision nodded. "Good. Then I'll talk to that time machine about getting my people back."

Agent Stardis waved her team forward. The agents started marching the cartel criminals to the I.L.E.A. ship, which was stationed a kilometer away through the arctic terrain.

Commander Vision watched them disappear into the gusting snow. When he lost sight of them, he turned toward the time device. The ribs still glowed in various shades of a bright white-blue.

"All right, it's time to get some answers," Vision told Spoor and Impact. "Let's move out."

The Bug Team members stomped through the snow toward the structure. The commander's expression was rigid, but it wasn't from the cold. Three of his people had been sucked into some sort of hole in time, and he was determined to pull them out of it.

Bug Team Alpha arrived outside the ancient structure and looked up at the dozens of temporal displays. They walked along the perimeter of the structure, searching for the single window where they had last seen their friends.

As they searched they saw images of people — humanoid and others — who were in other times and on other planets. They saw deserts and jungles, advanced civilizations, and prehistoric tribes. There were tropical cities and arctic ice-block shelters. The Bug Team couldn't help but be amazed by the diversity.

"There are so many times and places," Spoor noted.

"But why?" Vision wondered out loud.

"Query received," the machine's voice boomed. "Multiple locations were needed to transport this planet's population."

"Everyone on the planet was transported?" Vision repeated in surprise. He stopped and stared up at the structure as Impact and Spoor continued the search. "Why?"

"Imminent planetary destruction" the voice replied.

Commander Vision's spine went cold. The moment he heard the words *imminent* and *destruction*, his mind went into combat mode.

"How long until planetary destruction?" Vision demanded. He was already getting ready to message Stardis about the new threat. "Give me a countdown!"

"Planetary destruction is in twenty thousand local solar years," the machine replied.

"Twenty thousand?" Vision gasped in relief. Then he glared at the metal structure. "That's what you consider imminent?"

"In a planet's lifespan, yes," the voice responded. "This world lost its molten core. The surface has cooled. Soon no living things will be able to survive here. The population chose to move to different worlds and times."

"Commander! We found Radar, Locust, and Hopper!" a shout came from a few meters away.

"I'll have more questions for you in a minute, machine," Vision said and then sprinted along the outside of its glowing ribs. He did not notice that the glow had begun to fade.

CHAPTER 8

Lieutenant Radar walked as regally as possible behind a nervous servant through the Murasaki clan war camp. The perimeter guards had mistaken her for her ancestor, Princess Akiko, and let her through. The bluff was working so far. Radar, Hopper, and Locust were safe inside the camp, along with several soldiers they had rescued from the battlefield.

The servant led them toward the medical area of the camp. It was marked by a fence made from large sheets of cloth stretched between wooden poles. Inside, the Bug Team saw dozens of wounded soldiers stretched out on straw mats. The men whom the Bug Team had rescued collapsed in relief the moment they entered the medical area.

With the injured soldiers taken care of, Radar dismissed the camp servant. Then she quickly hustled her teammates out of sight behind a large tent.

"We're safe for now," Radar said as she removed the bandage on Locust's wound. "We need to start figuring out how to get back to our own time. Each moment we're here, there's a higher chance we'll affect the timeline."

"But we don't know how we were transported in the first place. Ow!" Locust gasped. Radar had begun using a medical device from her pack to remove the musket ball from his leg.

"Um, vortex," Hopper reminded them.

"It seems the likely cause," Radar agreed. "But how do we re-create it?"

"I have a theory," Professor Liin said as he walked around the corner of the tent.

Liin was not in his samurai disguise, but Hopper was so startled that he leaped into the air.

"Don't do that!" Hopper demanded.

"Oh! Sorry. I thought you'd want to hear about my findings as soon as possible," Liin said. He pulled out a computer tablet and started bringing up his data.

"What findings?" Radar asked without looking up. She was busy applying a skin adhesive to close Locust's wound. She wrapped his leg with a fresh bandage.

"I went back to my university and searched the archives for a temporal vortex that matched your description," Liin said. "It took me almost a month."

"A month?" Locust repeated, surprised. "You've been gone a month?"

"It hasn't been a month here, of course," the professor replied. "I simply used the temporal coordinates of our last encounter, and adjusted them to return just after we separated on the hillside. Then I tracked you here. Your temporal energy residue is quite . . . rare."

"How rare?" Radar asked.

"Only one planet in our records used this type of energy. But that world was abandoned twenty thousand years ago," Liin explained. "It was called Ramadandus."

"Rama 3! That's where we came from!" Hopper said, bouncing on his grasshopper footpads.

"Yes, but *when* did you come from?" the professor muttered to himself. He punched in numbers on his computer tablet. "I have to make some calculations."

"*Akiko Hime! Akiko Hime!*" The Bug Team suddenly heard shouts from nearby.

"Calculate fast," Radar said. "My family history is about to catch up with me."

"Can't you just time jump us out of here?" Locust asked the professor.

"No, that's quite impossible. The temporal energies don't match," Liin replied. "Whatever device sent you here is the only one that can get you back."

"I don't remember seeing a device, only the vortex," Radar said.

"Wait. What about that giant metal structure over the cartel base?" Hopper suggested. "It was glowing right before we were transported."

"You think that old thing could have been a time machine?" Radar asked doubtfully.

"Did it look like this?" the professor asked. He showed them an image on his tablet.

The Bug Team was amazed to see a shiny rib cage-like structure arching over a green landscape. There was no snow and ice, but the structure was unmistakable.

"That's it," Hopper said.

"Hmm. Interesting. I'm going to have to do some more research," Professor Liin said. "I'll catch up with you later."

"Wait, can you —" Radar started.

But the professor touched a small device on his wrist and blinked out of the timeline. A moment later a samurai came around the corner of the tent.

"*Akiko Hime!*" the warrior said in relief when he saw Radar. He bowed deeply at the waist. "We have been looking for you! Your uncle requests your presence."

Radar returned the bow. Locust and Hopper followed her example.

"Take us to him," Radar said.

The samurai eyed Hopper and Locust. Even with the disguises, they were an unusual sight.

"They are my bodyguards," Radar stated. "They will come with me."

"*Hai!* Yes!" the samurai said, bowing again. He led them from the medical area and farther up the hill.

With every step, Radar knew that the Bug Team was treading on history. One wrong move could change the future — her personal future, the future of Earth, even the existence of the Coalition. Claiming to be Princess Akiko seemed like a good idea at the time, but it could also have been a huge mistake.

The small group soon reached a clearing with a wide view of the battlefield. In the middle of the clearing was a large wooden platform covered by a three-sided tent. Samurai dressed in all sorts of elaborate armor surrounded a man seated on a simple campstool. His armor was the most spectacular of all. Radar recognized it instantly. It was displayed in her ancestral home on Earth.

"Murasaki Akira!" she whispered in awe.

The man looked up as if he had heard his name. "Akiko-san?" he said in shock. He stared at Radar's dirt-smeared face and mismatched armor.

Radar fell to her knees. She removed her helmet and bowed her forehead to the ground. Locust and Hopper did the same.

"*Ojisan!* Uncle!" Radar replied humbly. Even though the man was Radar's many-times great grandfather, Radar was pretending to be Princess Akiko. And this was the princess's uncle. "*Gomennasai!*"

To Radar's great surprise, General Murasaki Akira came down off the platform to Radar. He took her hands and gently lifted her to her feet.

"I am glad you're safe! But what are you doing here? I thought you were at the royal palace in Kyoto," Akira said. Then his face went pale. "Has something happened to the emperor?"

Radar's stomach clenched. She wondered what she had gotten herself into by taking on this identity. But as far as she remembered, the Battle of Sekigahara wasn't about overthrowing the emperor.

"The emperor is safe," Radar replied.

"Then why have you come here? Why have you put yourself in such danger?" Akira asked.

"I wanted to be with you, Akira-san," Radar said. Then she couldn't help herself and added, "I wanted to be like you."

Her statement was true enough. Radar had always wanted to honor the legacy of her many-times great grandfather. Tales of his bravery and brilliance in battle inspired her as a young girl.

The general chuckled. "You've always had a great imagination. But this is the real world." He patted Radar on the cheek as if she were a child. "The battlefield is too dangerous for a delicate flower like you."

Lt. Radar held in a groan of frustration. She knew Murasaki Akira wasn't talking about her, personally, but it felt that way. She was a member of Bug Team Alpha! She had been on missions these men could not imagine. She had training and abilities far beyond any of them — which was why she was the first one to react to the incoming attack.

CHAPTER 9

On Rama 3, Commander Vision ran up to Impact and Spoor. The two soldiers stood looking at one of the temporal displays.

"We found Radar, Locust, and Hopper," Spoor said. "It looks like they found some native garb."

Vision gazed up at the display. It was like a window on the past. There was no sound, only images. They watched their teammates bow before armored soldiers.

"Th-those are samurai!" Impact blurted in surprise.

"What's a samurai?" Spoor asked.

Impact gave her a disbelieving look.

Spoor shrugged. "Hey, I'm from Amaranth. We don't study much ancient Earth history."

"Samurai were the elite fighting force of Japan, an old Earth country," Commander Vision explained.

"Their culture invented some of the hand-to-hand combat skills we use today."

"They're also Radar's ancestors," Impact added.

Spoor nodded at the display. "It looks like she's meeting a few right now."

All of a sudden the scene erupted with confusion. People were shouting. Radar tackled a warrior to the ground. Hopper leaped over a line of samurai. Locust buzzed into the air. Then the temporal display sputtered and started to disappear.

"What's happening?" Vision shouted. "Bring my people back now, machine!"

"Unable to retrieve travelers. Power levels must be at twenty-five percent for retrieval," it replied. "Power is dropping. Current levels are at twenty percent."

Vision finally noticed the glow was fading on the metal ribs. "Is there any way to get the power back up?"

"Twenty-five percent can be reached by an outside energy boost," the machine replied.

"How *big* of an energy boost?" Vision asked.

The machine stated an energy output that startled the commander. If his large bug eyes could have gone wide, they would have.

"That's a lot of firepower," Vision said. He set his gaze on the eighteen weapons warehouses that still stood beneath the structure. "And that's probably what was produced when we blew up those two warehouses."

"We could blow up a couple more," Impact suggested.

"But how do we get to them? The last guys who tried to go through the grid were tossed back in time," Spoor reminded them.

"We ask," Vision said. "Machine, how do we pass through the temporal grids?"

"Walk," the machine replied simply.

Impact snorted. "This thing has an attitude."

Vision tried again. "So, we can pass through the grid without being transported to another time?"

"Correct," the machine said. "Power levels are not high enough for temporal transport."

"I guess it can't send or receive," Spoor said. She marched boldly toward the faltering energy grid.

"Wait!" Commander Vision ordered. Spoor stopped mid-step. "Neither of you are going through. I am."

Vision gazed at the window that showed the Battle of Sekigahara. "If I get through to the warehouses, you can follow me. If I don't, at least I can help Radar and the rest. Maintain your position."

"That could be a long time, sir," Spoor cautioned as she watched the grid flicker in and out.

The commander headed toward the temporal window. He saw flashes of combat. Vision shouldered his blaster, ready for whatever happened next. Then he stepped through the display.

On Earth, Lt. Radar caught a suspicious movement out of the corner of her eye. Her antennae were bound behind a scarf, but she didn't need their vibration-sensing abilities to notice danger.

"Bug Team! Incoming!" Radar shouted.

A squad of figures dressed in black rushed out of the forest and into the tent. They tossed shuriken — small, bladed throwing stars. *THUNK! THUNK!* In a matter of seconds, dozens of the snowflake-shaped weapons struck samurai armor.

"Ninja!" General Murasaki exclaimed.

Radar instinctively tackled the general to protect him. They hit the ground just as sharp shuriken flew where the general's head had been.

Hopper used his enhanced legs to leap over a line of Murasaki samurai. He smashed his large footpads into three ninja. They fell in a tangle of black-clad arms and legs.

Locust buzzed into the air. He fired his blaster and stunned the ninja with the skill of a sharpshooter. The attack was over in less than a minute.

The samurai rushed to tie up the would-be assassins. As Radar rolled off of General Murasaki, her scavenged armor fell apart. It revealed her advanced Talo-Titanium gear underneath. The general was stunned at the sight. So were the rest of the Murasaki warriors. But they were even more surprised by the sight of Hopper and Locust landing next to "Princess Akiko."

As the two Bug Team members helped Radar to her feet, they knew that there was no use trying to hide anymore. Hopper and Locust pulled off their samurai disguises.

The samurai stared at the soldiers' bug DNA enhancements. "*Kami!*" a warrior exclaimed.

The word echoed in Radar's memory. She remembered one of her family stories. According to legend, her ancestor General Murasaki had almost been assassinated by ninja. His life was saved by kami spirits. She had thought it was fantasy, an exaggerated fairy tale told to entertain children. But now she realized there was truth in those legends — Bug Team Alpha was the kami in her family's old stories of Sekigahara!

The Bug Team members weren't interfering in the timeline. They had always been a part of it. Radar decided to embrace her role in history.

The lieutenant pulled the scarf from her brow and revealed her bug antennae. The samurai gasped in awe. "Yes! We are kami," she announced. "We have come to bring the Murasaki clan luck on the battlefield."

Radar knew it would be best if the warriors believed she was a kami too. It would save the real Princess Akiko from awkward questions later.

Akira laughed. "You already have! You saved my life. That is a good start! Your actions will be remembered in the stories we tell of this day."

Radar bowed low.

"You are not such a delicate flower after all," the general added with a smile. Then he turned to his samurai. "Come! The spirits are with us! We will have victory on the fields of Sekigahara!"

General Murasaki led his cheering warriors down the hill. They were ready to test their good luck on the battlefield. The soldiers shoved the captured ninja ahead of them as they rushed forward.

The Bug Team was left standing by themselves. Suddenly Professor Liin popped into the timeline.

Hopper jumped back in surprise. "Stop doing that!" he complained.

"I've found the way to get you back to your own time," the temporal scholar said, ignoring Hopper's protest. "But you might not like it."

"Why not?" Radar asked.

"Because it involves a rather large explosion," Professor Liin replied.

Locust shrugged. "Explosions don't scare us."

"This might change your mind," the professor warned. "There's no temporal control device here to use. Nothing like the rib cage structure on Rama 3.

However, there is a bit of temporal energy left in your bodies. It's too weak to transport you. But a large explosion will re-energize it and create a vortex to send you back to where — and when — you came from."

"How big of an explosion?" Radar asked.

Liin showed the Bug Team the calculation on his tablet. The soldiers' eyes went wide.

The professor cleared his throat. "Also . . . you have to be standing in the middle of it."

CHAPTER 10

Commander Vision stood before the sputtering temporal display. It showed the images of Radar, Locust, and Hopper fighting black-clad figures. Vision, Impact, and Spoor wanted to help their teammates. But their teammates were on a different planet, hundreds of years in the past.

Vision's grip tightened on his blaster, and he stepped into the wavering images of battle. He passed through them like they were ghosts.

The commander exhaled. He hadn't realized he had been holding his breath. It was true — the machine's power levels were too low to transport. "OK. Impact, Spoor, come on through."

Getting past the temporal grid turned out to be the easy part. Getting to the weapons warehouses was hard.

When the ice had fallen from the metal structure, it had landed in giant shards. Now huge chunks of ice covered the ground in jagged heaps. The Bug Team members carefully climbed over the slippery pieces toward the warehouses.

"Impact, take one of the eastern warehouses. Spoor, take one in the southwest. I'll take one on the west side," the commander said. "Remember — abort if you see chemical weapons."

"Yes, sir," Spoor and Impact replied.

Suddenly blaster fire erupted all around them. The Bug Team immediately dropped for cover.

"Well, now we know where those missing cartel members are," Vision grumbled.

"The ones from the siege shelter?" Impact asked.

"They must have seen us go through the grid," Spoor said. "Then they decided to do the same thing."

The commander shielded his large eyes from the flying chips of ice. Then he counted the body-heat signatures running among the warehouses.

"I count eight of them. It has to be the pair from the shelter, plus the six who went missing after the ice fell. They've regrouped," Vision realized.

Impact gripped her blaster. "Three bugs against eight creeps. No contest," she declared.

Vision scanned the buildings. "The enemy is all gathered in one spot. A building in the northeast corner," he noted.

"Good. Does that mean we can blow up everything else?" Impact asked.

"As long as we get the energy boost we need, I'm fine with that plan," Vision agreed.

Impact grinned and saluted crisply.

"Break," the commander ordered.

Impact, Spoor, and Vision split up and headed toward three different warehouses.

On Earth, Radar and her teammates stood in an open field. They were about a kilometer away from the clashing samurai armies, but the team could still hear the tremendous uproar of the battle.

They had snuck out of the Murasaki war camp after the general had charged off with his troops.

Professor Liin took Radar and Hopper on his android warhorse in the opposite direction. Locust flew above and picked a location to carry out their plan.

"This is a good spot," Professor Liin said, looking around. "It's open and far from any humans. No one will accidentally get caught by the explosion or the vortex."

Radar, Locust, and Hopper finished arranging a wide ring of grenades and backup power packs on the ground. They walked to the center.

"This makes me very uncomfortable," Hopper admitted. He nervously bounced on his footpads.

"You have nothing to fear. My calculations are correct," Liin assured them.

"Easy for you to say. You're not standing where we're standing," Locust muttered.

"Don't worry. The energy released from the explosion will boost the temporal residue in your bodies and instantly form the vortex. It will protect you," the professor replied.

"If this works, will we return to the exact moment we left?" Radar asked.

Liin nodded. "Yes."

"There were giant chunks of ice falling on us at the time," Radar said. She looked at her teammates.

"Better set blasters on full," Locust added as he and Hopper braced themselves.

Radar tapped her wrist computer and got ready to trigger the explosions. "Goodbye, professor. You should pop into our timeline sometime," she said.

"Who says I haven't already?" he replied with a wink. He got onto his horse and galloped to a safe distance.

As the Bug Team watched him go, they also saw a line of mounted samurai galloping in their direction. Radar recognized the banners. A group of Murasaki warriors led by General Murasaki were chasing enemy deserters.

Radar watched in alarm. If the general or any of his troops got too close, they would be caught in the blast. They would either end up dead, or transported into the future. Both outcomes were unacceptable. Both possibilities would change the timeline.

Radar saw the general catch sight of her and wave to his magical kami spirit. She waved back. Then she pressed the trigger.

BAAAADOOOOOM!

The ring of grenades and power packs exploded. An instant later, General Murasaki watched as a blinding blue swirl appeared and lifted the kami spirits into the air. The warriors' horses reared in fright. By the time the samurai got their mounts back under control, the vortex was gone. All that remained was a ring of burned grass.

"*Kami!*" the general whispered in awe.

BAALAAAAM!

KAABOOOOM!

BAAWOOOOM!

On Rama 3, a trio of weapons warehouses exploded. Commander Vision and his team felt the impact of the blasts even from behind safe cover beyond the metal structure. As soon as the sound of the explosions faded, the commander leaped up. The ribs of the time machine were once again glowing bright blue.

"It worked!" Vision said, running toward the structure. No enemy blaster fire tried to stop him.

The commander ran up to the temporal window that displayed Lt. Radar and her team. They were standing in the middle of a field. Suddenly a huge explosion erupted around them.

"What was that? Machine, retrieve my people!" Vision shouted.

"Temporal coordinates recognized. Retrieval in progress," the machine replied calmly.

A bright vortex formed just inside the metal perimeter. When it faded, Vision's missing teammates stood in a large circle of melted ice. The soldiers immediately aimed their weapons above their heads.

"Hold your fire!" the commander ordered.

Radar, Locust, and Hopper looked surprised. They had expected falling ice. Instead, they saw destroyed warehouses and chunks of shattered ice littered across the ground.

"Well, this isn't exactly when we started, but I'm not going to complain," Hopper said.

All around them the glowing ribs of the metal structure dimmed. The energies turned from white-blue to yellow, and then to red. The temporal windows disappeared. The energy grids deactivated. It was safe for Commander Vision to run past the grid to his team. Impact and Spoor were right behind him.

"Are you all right?" Vision asked.

"Just a scratch," Locust replied as he patted his bandaged leg.

"It looks like you were busy," Radar said as she gazed at the wrecked warehouses.

Impact grinned. "The time machine needed a power boost to get you back here. We had to blow some stuff up to do it."

"That's what we did too," Hopper said. "Except we had to be standing in the *middle* of the explosion."

Vision scanned the ribs of the metal structure with his special spectrum-sensing abilities. The glow was fading fast.

"Machine! What are your power levels?" the commander asked.

"Power levels are at ten percent and dropping," the machine replied.

"Is there a way to boost it? Can we stabilize you?" Vision wanted to know.

"Negative. Shutting down," the device said.

"Quick, transfer your operating system to my wrist computer," the commander instructed. "We can save you. There's so much we could learn!"

"The interface does not match my system. Transfer is impossible," the machine said. Its voice weakened to a whisper. "Goodbye."

The metal ribs stopped glowing. They became cold and lifeless, just as they were when the Bug Team had first seen them. A chill wind spun the snow around the teammates in a weak vortex.

"It's going to be hard for General Barrett to believe our mission report on this one," Locust muttered.

"It's not over yet," Commander Vision reminded them. "We still have to round up the cartel members hunkered down in that northern warehouse. Let's go finish the job."

Reunited, Bug Team Alpha moved out.

Radar let out a happy sigh. "Back to normal," she said.

"How does it feel to be a plain old lieutenant again and not a princess?" Hopper asked.

"I was a princess *and* a kami spirit," Radar reminded him. "But it was amazing to see my ancestors in action and be a part of that history, even though I kept trying to stay out of it."

"I guess you were always meant to play a part. The kami stories wouldn't exist if we hadn't been there," Locust said. "In fact, General Murasaki might have died if it wasn't for you."

"So, if we hadn't been there and the general did die, would Radar never have been born? But then, how did she exist in the first place to go back in time to save him . . ." Hopper trailed off. He shook his head and groaned. "Ugh, time travel theory makes my head hurt."

Radar and Locust laughed as they trudged through the heavy snow. The Bug Team Alpha members moved further into the base, ready to complete their mission.

No one noticed the figure off in the distance. Hidden by the swirling snow and a camouflaged thermal suit, Professor Liin watched the special ops soldiers and took temporal readings on his tablet.

Mission Report

TOP SECRET AND CONFIDENTIAL

TO: GENERAL JAMES CLAUDIUS BARRETT, COMMANDER OF COLONIAL ARMED FORCES

FROM: COMMANDER JACKSON "VISION" BOONE, BUG TEAM ALPHA

SUBJECT: AFTER ACTION REPORT

MISSION DETAILS:

Mission Planet: Rama 3

Mission Parameters: Shut down Starkshadow cartel illegal weapons operation. Joint mission with Interplanetary Law Enforcement Agency [I.L.E.A.].

Mission Team: Bug Team Alpha [BTA]

* Commander Jackson "Vision" Boone
* Lt. Sancho "Locust" Castillo
* Lt. Anushka "Spoor" Kumar
* Lt. Irene "Impact" Mallory
* Lt. Akiko "Radar" Murasaki
* Lt. Liu "Hopper" Yu

MISSION SUMMARY:

BTA and I.L.E.A. engaged Starkshadow cartel in north polar region of Rama 3. Starkshadow base shielded by metal structure covered with ice. BTA detonated two warehouses in order to destroy ice roof and remove danger of falling debris. Energy from explosion activated an unknown function of the metal structure — time travel. Radar, Locust, and Hopper were caught in a temporal vortex and transported into the past. Further engagement with Starkshadow cartel delayed teammate rescue. Actions by Spoor and Impact led to capture of hostiles, allowing BTA to focus on rescue effort. Intelligent interface on time machine instructed BTA on how to retrieve teammates. Second series of explosions provided energy boost needed to bring back Radar, Locust, and Hopper. After retrieval, time machine shut down permanently. With full BTA force, remaining Starkshadow operatives were captured with little resistance.

ADDITIONAL REPORT --
LT. AKIKO "RADAR" MURASAKI:

Lt. Locust, Lt. Hopper, and Lt. Radar transported by temporal vortex to the year 1600 AD (Old Calendar) on Earth. Location identified as Battle of Sekigahara, in Japan. BTA members attempted to remain unnoticed in order to preserve timeline. Results were semi-successful. Radar was forced to assume identity of a royal family ancestor from the era to avoid conflict with samurai.

Unexpected contact was made with temporal scholar Professor Liin of Waazda University. His expertise allowed BTA to activate temporal energy residue in their bodies through planned explosion. Energy formed a transport vortex. Return to Rama 3 and present time successful.

APPENDIX 1: EQUIPMENT REQUISITION
Thermal components for Talo·Titanium armor
Covert transport ships [2]

APPENDIX 2: PARTICIPANTS
Bug Team Alpha [mission participants listed above]
Commander Lyra Stardis, I.L.E.A.
I.L.E.A. combat squad

END REPORT

Glossary

abort (uh-BORT)—to bring something to an early end

breach (BREECH)—to make a gap by using force

carapace (KAYR-ah-pays)—thick, protective shell that covers the back

cavalry (KA-vuhl-ree)—a unit of soldiers who travel and fight on horseback

combatant (KOM-bat-uhnt)—someone who takes part in a battle or fight

fortified (FOR-tuh-fyed)—having added protections against an attack

imminent (IM-uh-nuhnt)—about to happen

pike (PIKE)—a long, heavy spear

residue (REZ-uh-doo)—a usually small amount of something that remains after a process is completed

temporal (TEM-per-uhl)—having to do with time

thermal (THUR-muhl)—having to do with heat or holding in heat

vortex (VOHR-tex)—a spinning mass that pulls things toward its center

About the Author

Laurie S. Sutton has been interested in science fiction ever since she first saw the *Sputnik* satellite speed across the night sky as a very young child. By twelve years old, she was reading books by classic sci-fi authors Robert Heinlein, Isaac Asimov, and Arthur C. Clarke. And then she discovered *STAR TREK*.

Laurie's love of outer space has led her to write *STAR TREK* comics for DC Comics, Malibu Comics, and Marvel Comics. From her home in Florida, she has watched many Space Shuttle launches blaze a trail though the sky. Now she watches the night sky as the International Space Station sails overhead instead of *Sputnik*.

About the Illustrator

Patricio Clarey was born in Argentina and studied Fine Arts, specializing in illustration and graphic design. After graduating, he moved to Barcelona, Spain, where he's worked as a conceptual artist, book cover illustrator, and art director of a magazine. He also illustrates graphic novels and is the artist and coauthor of *Archeologists of Shadows*. Patricio's work has been featured in several publications, including Ballistic Publishing's *Exposé 9* and *Exposé 11*, which showcase some of the best digital art from around the world.

Discussion Questions

1. Impact challenged Commander Vision's order to fall back after she and Spoor failed to breach the cartel's siege shelter. What do you think of her decision? What would you have done in her place? Be sure to support your answer with evidence from the story.

2. In your own words, summarize why Radar was worried about being in the past. Do you agree with her concerns? Why or why not?

3. The members of Bug Team Alpha work together in order to tackle the toughest missions. Discuss at least two examples from the story where they used teamwork to overcome a challenge. Why do you think teamwork is important for a group like the Bug Team?